THE CHRONICLES OF NARNIA

THE VOYAGE OF THE DAWN TREADER

The Movie Storybook

First published in Great Britain in 2010 by HarperCollins Children's Books.
HarperCollins Children's Books is a division of HarperCollins Publishers,
77-85 Fulham Palace Road, Hammersmith, London W6 8JB

www.harpercollins.co.uk

www.narnia.com

ISBN: 978-0-00-736622-4

1 3 5 7 9 10 8 6 4 2

Printed in Italy

·THE CHRONICLES OF· NARNIA
THE VOYAGE OF THE DAWN TREADER
The Movie Storybook

Adapted by Coralie Noakes

Based on the screenplay by Christopher Markus, Stephen McFeely and Michael Petroni

Based on the book by C. S. Lewis

Directed by Michael Apted

HarperCollins *Children's Books*

Lucy and Edmund had been sent to Cambridge to stay with their aunt, uncle and rather unpleasant cousin, Eustace. Their father was fighting in the war and had gone to America, along with their mother and older sister, Susan. Their brother, Peter, was studying hard for his exam and couldn't join his brother and sister.

As they settled in, they spotted an interesting painting of a ship on the bedroom wall.

"It's very Narnian looking," said Lucy to Edmund. "It looks like the water's actually moving."

"What rubbish!" said Eustace, appearing at the door. "That's what happens when all you read are fanciful fairytales."

Suddenly, a big wave swept out of the picture and filled the room! Then the water sucked the trio into the picture and they found themselves in the ocean. A ship came towards them and the crew pulled them from the water.

To their amazement, one of the crew was Caspian!

"Behold our castaways - their majesties, Edmund the Just and Lucy the Valiant - high King and Queen of Narnia," said Caspian, introducing them to Captain Drinian and the crew.

Just then, they were interrupted by Eustace screeching.

"Get that thing off me!" he said, pushing Reepicheep away.

Lucy and Edmund were delighted to see their old friend, Reepicheep, but Eustace wasn't used to large, talking mice and thought he must be dreaming!

When Tavros the minotaur appeared, poor Eustace went speechless and fainted, so he was taken for a lie down.

Caspian explained they were on a ship called the Dawn Treader. He gave Lucy and Edmund some Narnian clothes. Then Caspian handed Lucy her dagger and healing cordial, and gave Edmund the torch he had accidentally left behind the last time he was in Narnia.

He then told them how, before he had taken the throne, his Uncle Miraz got rid of seven lords, who were friends of his father, by sending them off to explore the unknown Eastern Seas beyond the Lone Islands. The lords had not been seen since. He and his crew were now on a quest to find them.

Lucy went to check on Eustace and found a Faun offering him some soup.

"Mother? Why does mother smell like a goat?" asked Eustace.

"You're delirious," laughed Lucy.

She secretly poured some magic healing cordial into his water and Eustace began to feel much better, but didn't admit to it, of course.

Later, Lucy was staring down at the shimmering ocean, when she saw something moving. Suddenly, a beautiful water spirit leapt from the water! The spirit smiled and beckoned to Lucy before disappearing in the wind, leaving Lucy to wonder whether she had seen her at all.

The ship reached the Lone Islands, which seemed eerily deserted. Caspian, Lucy and Edmund headed off towards the castle. Inside they found a book filled with the names of villagers who had been sold as slaves.

Suddenly, hooded men appeared, daggers clenched in their teeth. Caspian, Lucy and Edmund tried to fight them off. Then there was a high-pitched scream. A huge man named Pug was holding a dagger to Eustace's throat! Caspian, Lucy and Edmund were forced to drop their swords. Pug gave the order for Eustace and Lucy to be taken to market. Edmund and Caspian were sent to a cell.

The next morning, a wagon full of slaves was driven out of the castle, down to the quayside and loaded onto a boat. The boat drifted into the distance and completely vanished into the darkness.

Caspian and Edmund watched from their cell window, not believing their eyes. Their fellow prisoner explained that the slaves were being fed to the darkness to try and keep it away. He said that he and his lords had tried to find the source of the darkness, but the others never came back. He was the only one left and his courage had failed him. Caspian realised the prisoner was Lord Bern, one of the lords of Telmar.

Lucy was sold as a slave and it was Eustace's turn next! Suddenly, some slave traders stepped forward, pulling back their hoods. There was Reepicheep, standing on Captain Drinian's shoulders, and Tavros too!

"For Narnia!" they cried, charging forward and untying Lucy, Eustace and the other slaves.

Guards leading Caspian, Edmund and Lord Bern from their cell were distracted by the noise. Caspian and Edmund seized their chance and fought off the guards. Soon, villagers came out of hiding and joined in the fight. The slave traders were defeated!

Lord Bern revealed a sword that Caspian's father had given him. He gave the sword to Caspian, saying it was a gift from Aslan to protect Narnia. To Edmund's delight, Caspian handed the sword to him.

The ship set sail again. When it reached land, the crew decided to spend the night on shore and explore the island in the morning. Everybody was sleeping, when footprints appeared magically in the sand.

"Take her," said a voice, spotting Lucy's book and realising she could read.

An invisible hand clamped over Lucy's mouth. Lucy woke in fright to find herself being carried by invisible hands into the woods.

Lucy was dropped on a lawn. She pounced to her feet, gripping her dagger, but something invisible knocked it from her hand. Voices told Lucy to enter the mansion and recite the spell that makes the unseen seen. Lucy could see no mansion. Just then, an invisible door opened and a staircase appeared.

Lucy stepped through the magic door. She looked in every room, until she came to a library and found a huge book of spells. She spotted a beauty spell and couldn't resist trying it. The page became a mirror and Lucy suddenly looked like her sister, Susan!

"I'm beautiful!" she said, before returning to herself again.

She tore out the page and the book roared! Then the pages fluttered, landing on the spell to make the unseen seen.

Lucy read out the spell. Suddenly to her delight, she saw Aslan beside her!

"I have been here all the time," he said, "but you have just made me visible."

Lucy was ashamed when she realised that he'd seen her take the beauty spell. Just then, she heard footsteps. Aslan disappeared and a tall man with a long beard came towards Lucy.

"Your Majesty," he said, bowing. He was Coriakin the magician.

Meanwhile, the others had woken and realised Lucy had gone. They followed the footprints in the sand until they found Lucy's dagger. Suddenly, spears hemmed them in and their weapons were taken. Invisible creatures threatened them with claws, tusks and fangs! Then Lucy's spell started to work and the creatures were revealed. There were no claws, tusks or fangs, just tubby little creatures with huge feet, called Dufflepuds!

"This place just gets weirder," said Eustace.

The door to the mansion opened and Coriakin and Lucy appeared. Coriakin said he'd made the Dufflepuds invisible to protect them from the evil behind the darkness. He unrolled a magical map and pointed to Dark Island, where the evil lurked.

Coriakin told of a Narnian ship that passed through seven years ago with the Lords Revilian, Argoz, Mavramorn and Rhoop, and the man at Deathwater Island must be the Lord Restimar. So Caspian and the voyagers planned to set sail once again.

That night, Lucy tried out her beauty spell again and saw herself as Susan. She stepped through the magical mirror. Edmund and Peter were there, but they didn't know who Lucy was or anything about Narnia. Lucy panicked. Then she heard Aslan's voice and she was back as herself on the ship. Aslan told Lucy she shouldn't try to be someone else.

Stormy weather blew the ship off course and it arrived at Goldwater Island. Caspian, Lucy and Edmund searched for clues. They found an anchor with its rope dangling down a hole. Inside the hole was a beautiful grotto of emerald water. The trio went down to investigate.

There was a golden statue of a man lying at the bottom of the water. Edmund reached for it with a branch. A stream of gold slithered up the branch towards his fingers. He dropped the branch just in time. It had turned to gold! Then Edmund spotted a sunken shield. Caspian recognised it had the crest of Lord Restimar on it.

"Whoever has access to this pool could be the most powerful person in the world," said Edmund. "We'd be so rich, no-one could ever tell us what to do, or who to live with."

"You can't take anything out of Narnia, Edmund," warned Caspian.

The two of them started to fight and Lucy had to stop them.

"Can't you see what's happening? This place has tempted you. This is what Coriakin was talking about," said Lucy.

Meanwhile, Eustace was walking along a cliff, when the ground gave way and he fell. He found himself surrounded by jewels, and greedily grabbed at them. Suddenly, he came across a skeleton, half buried in the treasure. Eustace screamed. Then his greed got the better of him and he took the bejewelled armband from the skeleton's wrist.

Edmund and Caspian realised Eustace was missing and went to look for him. They found his clothes, scorched and torn to shreds!

"I should never have left him," cried Edmund. Then they saw the skeleton and Caspian saw from its shield that this was Lord Octesian.

Then there was a horrifying shriek and flames rose out of the valley. A giant dragon appeared and landed on the Dawn Treader! The ship tipped dangerously under its weight. The crew shot arrows, and the dragon shrieked and headed back to the island.

Caspian and Edmund ran back to the boat and the dragon flew towards them, grabbed Edmund in its claws and soared off. Edmund looked down and saw, burnt into the valley floor, huge letters which read 'I AM EUSTACE.'

"You have got to be joking!" yelled Edmund.

Eustace had been turned into a dragon! Eustace and Edmund returned to the shore.

"He was obviously tempted by the treasure," Edmund explained to the others.

The next morning, the ship set off again. There was no wind, so Eustace wrapped his dragon's tail around the ship and helped to tow it through the water. Eventually the ship arrived at Ramandu's Island. Caspian, Lucy and Edmund

led the crew through a dark wood until they reached a long stone table with
a banquet of food!

There were three figures at the table, with long grey hair and beards, sitting still as statues. It was Lord Revilian, Lord Argoz and Lord Mavramorn! Just then, a mist of breath came out of Lord Mavramorn's mouth. The men were alive, but under a spell. Caspian noticed the lords' swords were pointing to the centre of the table.

Suddenly, a blinding flash burst through the trees and a figure appeared out of the brilliant light. She was Liliandil, the daughter of Ramandu, and the most beautiful woman Caspian had ever seen.

Liliandil told everyone to help themselves to the banquet.

"These poor men were half mad by the time they reached our shores, ravaged by temptation," said Liliandil, pointing to the lords. "They were threatening violence upon each other. Violence is forbidden at the table of Aslan, so they were sent to sleep and can only be woken by..."

Then Liliandil led Caspian, Lucy and Edmund to a hilltop and pointed to the Dark Island.

"Before long, the evil will be unstoppable. The fate of Narnia depends on you," she said, before shooting back into the sky.

The crew set off towards the Dark Island.

"In case we don't get through this, I want you to know I think of you as my brother, Edmund," said Caspian.

"You, too. I'm sorry we argued," said Edmund.

Then a chilling moan came from a rock.

"Keep away!" said a man, waving a sword. The ship drew closer and as the terrified, elderly figure cowered in fright Caspian realised it was Lord Rhoop. Eustace swooped down and plucked Lord Rhoop off the rock.

"You shouldn't have come," said Lord Rhoop. He told them not to think of their worst fears or they would become reality.

Everyone tried hard, but it was too late. There was a chilling sound of something moving in the water.

"Edmund, what nightmare did you think of?!" cried Lucy.

Everyone turned to see a giant serpent rising out of the water. Edmund and Caspian tried to fight it off. Eustace, letting out a cowardly squawk, desperately tried to flee from the serpent but hit it clumsily. The serpent plunged into the sea with Eustace. When they surfaced, the serpent hurled Eustace into a rock. Lord Rhoop threw his sword into Eustace's side.

"No!" cried Caspian, Edmund and Lucy, as Eustace fled in pain.

Edmund led the serpent towards the front of the ship.

"Crush it on the rocks!" he called. Caspian steered the boat into the rocks, pinning down the serpent.

Lucy fell to her knees and closed her eyes.

"Aslan, if you ever loved us at all, send us help now," she said.

"Courage, dear heart," came the voice of Aslan. Lucy looked up to see an albatross hovering overhead.

Eustace collapsed in some shallow water, moaning and hurt. Suddenly, there was a bright light. Aslan appeared and helped turn Eustace into a boy again. Then there was a flash and Eustace appeared!

The serpent moaned in terror. The crew fired harpoons at it, harnessed it with ropes and pulled it onto the deck. Edmund looked it in the eyes. He plunged his sword into the serpent. The crew let go of the ropes and the serpent slid limply into the water.

Suddenly, the darkness lifted and light beamed down from the sky. The spell had lifted! Then a flotilla of Narnian boats came sailing towards them. It was the slaves that had been fed to the darkness! The crew of the Dawn Treader cheered and waved.

Eustace swam from the island towards the ship. Everyone was delighted to see him. "I'm a boy again!" he called happily.

"Eustace! My friend!" cried Reepicheep, jumping into the water.

Then Reepicheep pointed. The water was white and shimmering. A sea of lilies stretched to the horizon.

"Aslan's country," said Caspian. Edmund, Lucy, Caspian, Eustace and Reepicheep took a longboat towards the sea of lilies. There was an enormous wave in the distance.

The group walked across the sand and turned to see Aslan beside them. He told them that his country was beyond the wave. If they went there, they could never return.

"Is my father in your country?" asked Caspian.

"You can only find that out for yourself," said Aslan.

Caspian walked towards the wave, but turned back. "I can't imagine my father would be very proud that I gave up what he died for," he said.

Lucy and Edmund decided they must go home too. They loved it here, but they loved their family too. Then Reepicheep stepped forward and asked if he could go to Aslan's country and Aslan agreed. Reepicheep said goodbye to his friends and paddled towards the wave in a small boat. The boat rose to the top of the wave and disappeared in a flash of light.

Aslan reassured the children that he would always be watching them. "In your world I have another name," he said.

"Narnia owes you a great debt," said Caspian, as the children stepped through a gap in the wave.

They thrashed about in the water, then found themselves sitting in a puddle on the bedroom floor back in Cambridge!

Caspian and his crew all returned safely from Ramandu's Island and the three lords awoke.

Lucy, Edmund and Eustace spoke often of Narnia in the days that followed. After the war, Lucy and Edmund went back home and Eustace missed them with all his heart, and he knew all Narnians would do too, until the end of time.